THE SHADOW MASTER'S EYE

ANNI RATTEN

Voices of Today
Australia

Text and Illustrations © 2022 Anni Ratten
Published by Voices of Today with permission
Willetton, Western Australia

ISBN paperback: 9781953007865
ISBN eBook: 9781953007841
Also available as an audiobook from all good audiobook retailers.

Cover image © by Anni Ratten
Cover design by Voices of Today.

Let the tears flow, O ye people of the world
Weep for your salvation

– Robert Jordan
'The Wheel of Time'

What would life be if we had no cause to attempt anything.

– Vincent van Gogh

Contents

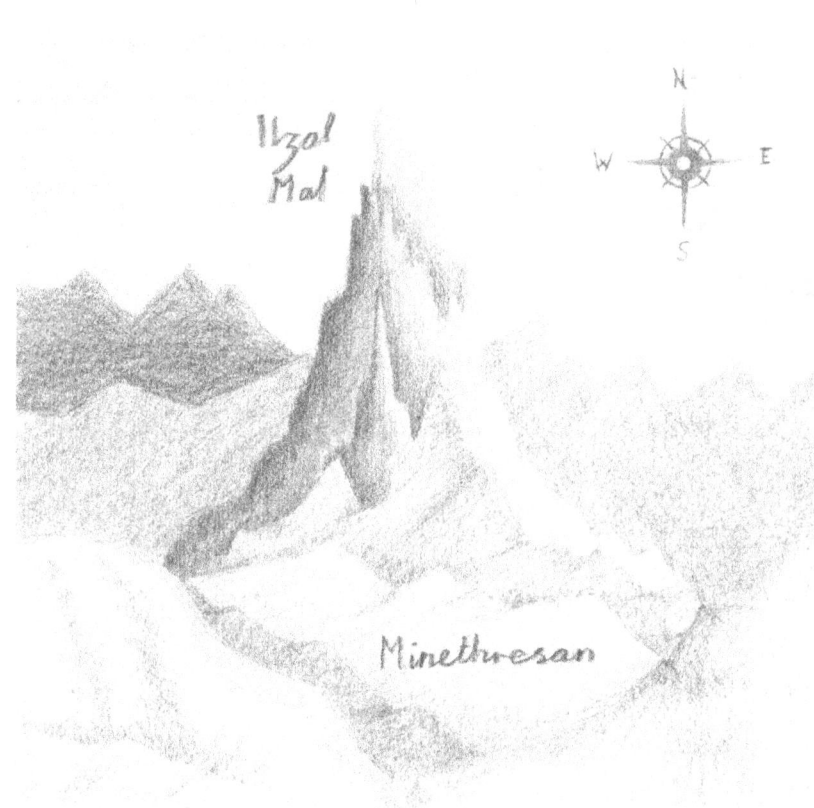

Ilzol Mal

Minethresan

Thanisveil

Thamisveil

ANNI RATTEN

PROLOGUE

The people of the Minethresan Valley lived in peace and harmony with each other and with the land. At no time did it cross their minds to wish for more. Life was good as it was. It was enough.

Regrettably, not all thought this way. One of the humans was not satisfied with life - he wanted more. His name was Uzma.

All knew the legend of the gem, called Bathamis, that lived in the mountain and would grant you ultimate power and control, but no one paid much attention to it. Who would want such things? Why disturb the peace of life?

However, Uzma was greedy and he followed the ancient legend of Bathamis. He ventured into the mountain and sacrificed his eye as the blood and flesh that would rouse the gem from its long dormancy. Only the fortitude to cut out a piece of one's self can invoke such a powerful weapon. It was said that the dearer to you the piece you gave up, the greater the power Bathamis would provide.

So the gem took on the form of Uzma's eye, but for what it gives, it always takes away. Bathamis ate away at his very being; body and soul. His spirit was expunged of all emotion and feeling but those of hunger for power and destruction. His form started to decay, entering the early stages of death. His mind was assailed by madness. Yet he lived on in his corpse. It was but a tool, a holder of the poison liquid that would soon spill forth and seep its way into firmer ground. There it could take root and spread its seeking tendrils throughout the world to disperse chaos and suffering. Soon he would cast the useless shell of a man's body aside and burst free to wreak havoc and rule over the world. Bathamis thrived on destruction and despair; fed on it and was strengthened by it.

As Uzma's evil influence grew, plants on the mountain struggled to grow, clouds covered the sky in an eternal gloom and the folk in the valley below toiled to gather sufficient food to feed themselves. Soon they started to starve, and they could no longer find happiness in living. Uzma also raided the weakened human community – just one or two at a time. However, if you stack enough seconds on one another, they become a year, and likewise, the numbers of the stolen gradually grew. Before long, the humans scattered, leaving everything behind. Little did they know how much that really was.

The folk of the valley became mere animals, tormented by terror and anguish. Many starved. Many went mad or killed themselves to escape the agony that life now harboured. These animals were but shadows of what they had once been. They were wretched, cadaverous excuses for humans. Like the dead, hauled from their graves to live again; the stuff of nightmares. They appeared to the eye to be bundles of sticks bound together by a clumsy child's hand to resemble humans and dressed in scraps of cloth.

But not only had their appearance changed, indeed their whole nature was altered. These creatures, the next generation, remembered nothing of their ancestors' lives. They knew neither light nor happiness, peace nor love. They had grown up in fear and despair. Over time, they were renamed, the Gwakas.

However, some Gwakas escaped the inevitable fate of so many left behind. While others perished or turned slave to the mountain, a group of Gwakas found the end of the mountain range. Here, far outside the immediate influence of Bathamis, the rabble that remained of the once thriving human civilisation, was able to build anew. They established cities, and, over time, a government. They thought, maybe, they had found a better life for themselves. So little did they know. So ignorant they were. They would never escape that easily.

ANNI RATTEN

CHAPTER 1
Gwaka

Neave was merely six when her father Aieron had died. No one knew for a fact how it had occurred or who was to blame. Her mother never talked about it − Neave suspected she did not know either − and Lewellyn (the closest thing Neave ever had to an uncle) who always appeared to know everything, was no help. She could guess, though. It was always the same ones behind the disappearances, never mind that no one discussed them. To do so would be to invite your own death.

Neave did not remember her father. She had wiped his presence from her mind and did not desire to recall. However, she believed she knew who had stolen him. Neave saw them every day, the soldiers, marching up and down the streets searching for those disobeying the government rules. The streets cleared when they appeared.

Most Gwakas in Neave's city (named Thamisveil) were helpless, wretched figures who could not imagine another life. The Gwaka government used this frailty in its citizens to keep the powerful position they held. Neave was one of the few whose ancestors had not travelled quite so far down the road to animalism. Her mother Mirrin had formed the Scholars – a group of men and women led by Mirrin – who knew the truth about the government. It was power hungry and merciless. How else could the government have disposed of her father and all the other Gwakas who had fallen into the mass graves outside the city. Neave could never forgive them for what they had taken from her. For what she could have had, and what her life could have been. How did they have the right to determine her destiny in that way?

Mirrin had formed the scholars in order to fight back. Her rebel group had grown to fifty members since the fateful day she had descended to Minethresan Valley, in defiance of the government.

It was not easy being a rebel. They were continuously in hiding and new recruits were rare because of the difficulty in finding those willing to fight for the Scholars' cause. It was also almost impossible to communicate. Group gatherings of four or more people were banned, and curfews made night meetings very dangerous. Government soldiers patrolled the streets around the clock and if you were discovered breaching any rules the gallows were ready and waiting for you.

Neave had never consorted with anyone outside the Scholars organisation, let alone other children. Babies were scarce among the Gwaka community. No one wanted children; they ate all the food and made life more burdensome than it already was. The few that were born were not treated well. No love was put into raising them and their gaunt, beaten features and haunted expressions confirmed insufficient sustenance and regular punishments. Children born were only there to ensure the population did not grow too small and fade out of existence. Neave was an exception to the rule. She had never been beaten in her life and her gauntness was normal for all Gwakas.

No one ever had enough food. Even the government officials were scrawny creatures with no mind for anything but eating, sleeping and obeying orders. The Scholars were different to the majority of Gwakas though, for they knew what they had lost, what they could have had. Most Gwakas did not know their origin and the emotions and culture of their previous lives were forgotten. Some did not even have names anymore. They were lost souls, existing solely to do what others said. Some richer Gwakas had shops where they sold produce to the wealthy who could afford such luxuries. They had slightly more freedom.

The poorest had no choice. For them it was either die of hunger or exist from the scraps they received through their labour. They laboured every day, all day. Neave would see them sometimes at dawn, chained together by their ankles, toiling in the fields or cleaning the ever-polluted city. At sunset they were handed rations for payment, (barely enough to keep them alive) before retiring to their shelters in The Outer City to sleep before the never-ending cycle of desolation started over again. If they lagged they were whipped.

The majority of poor Gwakas died from these labour duties. They went quietly, keeling over in their chains to sprawl face down in the mud. The soldiers would whip them to ensure they were dead and then cart them away to the mass graves. If you were lucky as a labourer, you might make it to your twentieth year.

The first time Neave had encountered this terrible show of cruelty she was barely seven years of age. It was the year after her father had disappeared and she was running an errand for her mother. It had taken her longer than usual to buy flour from Lewellyn; the prices were rising again, and the sun was sinking. She hurried back through the poorer section of the city, or she tried to. The mud in The Outer City was even worse than where she lived. It coated her from knee to toe and her feet squelched and stuck in the muck at every step. The houses in this section did not deserve the name. Most were made from salvaged scraps of wood, sheets of metal and strung up plastic; no windows or doors to keep out the cold wind. Lewellyn lived within The Outer City slums as a poor merchant. Neave's house, however, sat further within Thamisveil with the other richer merchant families. This meant, when visiting Llewellyn's shop, she had to brave the dangers of The Outer City to find her way home.

Some Gwakas stared at her out of their shelters as she went. Most did not care. They hunched over meagre bites of food or huddled in their blankets, struggling to retain some of their body heat. These Gwakas made Neave uneasy. They did not have any interest in what went on around them and many could no longer properly communicate through language. Neave suffered. Everyone suffered – but these Gwakas suffered the most. At least Neave's home had walls.

Those with still a spark of curiosity watched as she dashed on around a corner and almost ran into the back of a soldier. Neave stumbled back hurriedly and took in the scene. A line of about twenty labourers stood in the middle of the street, silently staring into the distance, except for one. A Gwaka was lying on the ground, unmoving. Neave did not understand. She was just about to continue past them, when one of the soldiers advanced on the fallen figure and produced a two-foot-long stick from his belt. It gave the impression of being made of leather until he wound the leather off into a thin strap that dragged on the ground. He lifted the whip over his head and brought it whistling through the air to fall on the prostrate Gwaka.

Neave gasped. The Gwaka was obviously injured and required help, but they whipped him. She wanted to scream, but there was a lump in her throat that prevented any sound. The lash fell again and again. Blood sprayed off the end of the leather strap and splattered everywhere. A droplet landed on Neave's cheek and she unconsciously wiped it off with her finger. She looked down at her hand to see a red smudge, (already beginning to dry) that just moments before, was the lifeblood of another being.

This time she did scream. It ripped through her throat, painfully, and crawled violently out of her mouth to announce another tormented being to the world.

One of the soldiers turned around, startled, and looked down at her in bewilderment. Neave, screaming with renewed strength, desperately stepped back, turned around, and ran for all she was worth. Neave was a good runner, as she had been running messages for her mother for the past year. She knew her way around the city and it was not too long before she reached the sanctuary of her home. She was no longer screaming. Instead the tears slid down her cheeks leaving runnels in the layers of grime that coated her face.

To this day, Neave remembers her mother's comforting arms around her and her reassuring voice as she recounted what she had experienced. When Neave had settled, her mother told her – for the very first time – the tale of her travels into Minethresan valley:

When I was sixteen I experienced a vivid dream about a Gwaka who sat on a log and told me to come to him in the valley under the mountain known by the name of Itzal Mal, or the Shadow Mountain. The scholars named it so because of its black hew and how it seemed eternally cast in shadow. This dream was branded onto my mind and with every passing day the urge to obey the Gwaka and go to him, grew stronger. Eventually I set out to find him.

My family thought me mad. To wander outside the city is to break the rules of the government, unless one has labour duties, and even then it was only allowed with an escort of guards. Also, my dream sounded to my family, like any ordinary dream about the Sage Gwaka. They shrugged it off, but I could not. The vision did not let me rest and so I left.

Neave knew the set of stories involving Sage Gwaka. They had always been some of her favourites. They were about a Gwaka who had lived for hundreds of years in a valley under a mountain. When Neave was very young she used to beg Lewellyn to tell them in front of the fire after dinner, on nights when the rebels had managed to meet. She would sit on Lewellyn's lap and look up at his earnest wrinkled face and watch his expressions as he told about the wise old Gwaka. She thought Lewellyn extraordinary. He was old and that in itself was a miracle. To be an elder in this world was an achievement to applaud. It signified that you had lived past your youth. But beyond that, Lewellyn could also tell stories like no other. He could make otherwise boring tales come to life before your eyes.

I found the valley and entered.

At this point in the story Mirrin fell silent and stared into the distance with a strange expression on her face that made the corners of her mouth do absurd things. Neave called to her impatiently to continue her story. For the remainder of the tale her mother looked at her with sadness pervading her countenance.

I found Sage Gwaka crouched on a log facing east. He told me unbelievable things about the Gwakas.

"You do not have a name for this valley," he said. "But it does have a name, and it was once known by all."

"What is it?" I asked.
"Minethresan."
"Minethresan," I echoed in wonder.
"Gwakas once lived here," he replied pensively. "They were a happy folk. They lived fully."
"What is happy, what does it mean?" I asked. "And who were these Gwakas?"
"You would not understand. Happiness, peace, joy, love, they

15

have been wiped from your memory," he said sadly. "And, as for who these Gwakas were?

They are you, you are them. But take heart my young one. Learning about your true past, your true ancestry will begin to set you free and this knowledge will allow you to feel joy and love again."

Mirrin then told Neave about the destruction of the humans by the government and why the Scholars had formed.

It is strange that such a small thing as a dream had the power to change a life in such a dramatic way. Neave shuddered to think what would have happened if her mother had not had her vision. Had not ventured to the valley and had not decided to start a rebellion. Would she be like one of those other Gwaka children, born only to reproduce, not acknowledged in any way, destined to work in chained lines and whipped whenever her strength waned? Would she have survived this long?

Years later, when Neave's own adventure had begun she would remember this tale and it would help her to discover the truth.

CHAPTER 2
Trapdoor

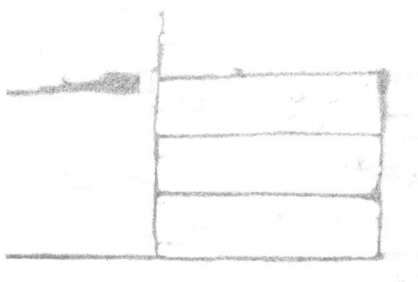

Trapdoor

It was Salvation Day and Neave was now sixteen years of age. On this day one hundred years ago, the Gwakas had fashioned the government. It was also the only labour free day for the entire year. It was supposed to be a day of celebration where all the Gwakas gathered in The City Square to listen to government officials make longwinded speeches about the importance of Salvation Day. Everyone was expected to be there, even the soldiers.

This latter piece of information is the important part. With no one in the streets and all soldiers off duty it was the perfect moment for the rebel Gwakas to gather in larger numbers. Salvation Day was Neave's favourite day of the year, not because it was a public holiday, but because it was the only time all the rebels met together in one place.

They avoided going to the same location two years running and on this occasion it was to be held at one of the richer Scholar's houses.

When all the Gwakas were marching in silence towards The City Square, Neave and her mother merged in with them. The soldiers herded the Gwakas and made sure no one trailed behind, checking houses for any stragglers.

Neave and her mother walked with the crowd until they came upon the narrow alleyway they had been looking out for. With her mother leading, Neave ducked into the alley and bolted down into the trapdoor Mirrin held open for her. Her mother followed and closed the lid quickly behind her, shutting off all remaining light.

"Is that you, Mirrin?" a voice asked from the darkness. It was Llewellyn.

"Indeed," Neave's mother replied. "Are we waiting on anyone else? Where's Brooke?"

"Brooke won't be joining us, she was executed three months ago, I saw them come and take her. She used to make me teas for my aching joints. Brooke was a good Gwaka, strong and always kind, even in the hardest of times."

An uncomfortable silence followed this statement that was eventually broken by soldier's boots pounding on the wooden planks overhead. Neave listened as their footsteps faded away. She was used to this routine by now, as it happened every year. They would hide in this hole until the last soldier patrol had past overhead, then double back towards the meeting spot.

Like every other year, Neave's mother checked for any remaining troops. When she waved the all-clear, Neave dashed out of the trapdoor and headed south, with Mirrin and Lewellyn beside her. After braving a few alleys and wide muddy streets they arrived at the arranged meeting place.

It was a large building made of wood with windows lining its face. The door was of sturdy timber, the doorknob iron.

Neave's mother walked up to it and knocked in a pattern that would let the door guard know it was a Scholar. A shutter opened on the side of the door and a nervous face peered through the crack.

"Mirrin," the Gwaka exclaimed. "And Lewellyn and Neave of course."

The face disappeared and the shutters closed. Soon Neave heard the jangle of keys and bolts sliding. The door opened to reveal a soft faced Gwaka with long limbs by the name of Linken. He was always lively and in good humour and ever had strange rumours to share.

"Another day another potentially deadly clandestine meeting of the vanguard," he said by way of a greeting, in his usual blithe manner. However, his smile was made a liar by his eyes, as they carried the seriousness of the moment in their glance.

He quickly ushered them inside, casting worried looks up and down the street. The annual rebel meeting was indeed a serious thing – and dangerous. Usually the Scholars were solitary and kept a very low profile. This was the only day in the year that they came out of hiding to gather in large numbers.

As Neave followed the others into the house, she glanced back to catch a closer look at the inside of the door. It had rectangles carved into its surface. Neave stared at this curiosity in wonder for several seconds before pulling herself together. She shut her mouth with a snap and shook her head in disbelief. Many Gwakas did not even own a door let alone one with carvings decorating it.

She turned away as Linken slid the bolts back into place. Neave left him standing guard over the door and hurried to catch up to Mirrin and Lewellyn. They entered a large room, at least four paces in length, and splitting at the seams with Gwakas crowded together in chairs or settled on cushions. In the centre of the room was a clear space of floor over which hung an oil lantern – a failed attempt to replicate a chandelier – yet more than Neave could ever have hoped for. She and her mother could barely afford candles.

Neave and her family were merchants, but poor ones, and this was her first time inside a rich trader's house. They were usually owned by those in favour with the government and located in the northern part of the city (called The High End), away from the severity of The Outer City and the mass graves. This house was an exception; being placed in the south.

They were some of the last to arrive and Neave squeezed in next to a Gwaka with dark hair and knobbly fingers to watch as Scholars moved aside to let her mother and Lewellyn into the centre of the room, beneath the chandelier.

Lewellyn was part of the council that helped make decisions for the Scholars. It consisted of three other Gwakas: Delyssius, Kimberly, and Morgan, along with her mother as the leader. The small number made it easier to meet on a regular basis.

This, however, was no ordinary meeting of the Scholars, where they would review the Scholars' numbers and make plans to recruit. This year they were here to discuss something of far greater importance: how to overthrow the government.

Lewellyn joined the other council members as Mirrin raised her hand for silence. She began to speak.

"This year," she began in a commanding tone, "we are not—"

She was interrupted by a tremendous smash at the door that almost rattled it off its hinges .

CHAPTER 3
Veiled Face

Veiled Face

All heads turned towards the left wall.

There came another smashing blow to the door. Everyone was on their feet at once, staring in its direction. The door shuddered and a crack, that seemed to split the air in two, emanated from its tortured frame. Neave watched as a fissure appeared down its centre. The Scholars were frozen as the door continued to groan from a heavy weight on the outer side and as splinters flew off in all directions.

Then suddenly there was commotion. Gwakas frantically scrambled for the windows. It was a desperate rush for escape.

Neave herself ran full pelt for the nearest window. She was shoved from all sides and could not make out her mother through the throng. She glanced over her shoulder and a terrible sight greeted her eyes. Scholars scampered as veiled figures burst through the splintered doorway. A spear flew through the air; thrown by the lead assailant. Neave made out a glint of blue in between the black cloth that covered the Gwaka's face, before the crowd jostled her about again. Instinct took control and she elbowed her way to a window, jumped over the sill and dropped to the ground on the other side. Without a thought, she dashed for one of the alleys opposite.

Once she reached the safety of the shadows cast by the two neighbouring houses, she turned and peeked her head around the corner, trying all the while to still her pounding heart. Neave watched as Gwakas poured out of the windows and surged down the streets.

She scanned the stream of bobbing heads for the familiar face of her mother. A figure ran past her alley entrance. She yelled carelessly, "Lewellyn!" Then she quickly clamped a hand over her mouth and retreated further into the alley, hoping no veiled attackers had heard. A moment later Lewellyn ducked into the alley .

"Neave, what are you doing here?" He asked, out of breath. "You can't stay here, it's too dangerous. They are after us; the government. We have to get back home and lay low. Where is Mirrin?"

"I don't know. I hoped you would know." Neave answered, alarmed. "I am staying here and waiting for her."

"You cannot wait here, please Neave, we need to go. She is probably already home."

Neave shook her head frantically and obstinately backed away.

"Neave, please." A note of desperation entered his voice and he rung his hands, wildly peering about him over his shoulder. Neave just gazed at him. "I'll search for her, and when I find her I will come back and get you, I promise." He said no more, but nodded to her and left, disappearing around the corner. *What is happening? Where is my mother?* Neave thought, as she squatted alone in the shadows.

Mirrin's side hurt, badly. She could not quite remember what had happened. It was all a blur.

The pain washed over her again. She had been standing to speak when the door came crashing down, to reveal veiled attackers. She had seen the leader of the party scan the Scholars with his eyes as the room broke into mayhem. It had all happened so quickly.

Next she knew, a searing pain had shot through her side and all had gone black.

Mirrin felt the blood dripping down her side. She would die soon of blood loss if she didn't get help. Just then she heard the scuff of feet from down the corridor. She managed to lift her head enough off the boarded floor to distinguish the figure walking towards her but had to blink several times before she could make out details through her tear-ridden eyes. He wore nondescript clothing and a black veil covered his face. He walked with a determined stride and held a dagger in his left hand.

She tried to cry out to him for help, but the words caught in her throat and only a low moan of despair escaped her lips.

The man crouched down beside her. She could just make out light blue eyes past the veil. *Do I know this man?* she wondered. She desperately tried to organise her thoughts, but the fog that reached into her mind obliterated all rational thinking; she could only watch as he came closer, knelt beside her and proceeded to remove the veil from his face to reveal a row of straight white teeth. *Why is he holding a knife?*

"I have been looking for you my dear," the stranger said in a rich voice, as he smiled, flashing those startling teeth. "The Shadow Master ordered me to personally see to your death. The others are already gone. Their instructions were to grab and run. I have

26

the privilege of special orders." *I know that voice, that smile.* Mirrin's eyes opened wide.

"You recognise me;' it was not a question. "I had to make sure of that."

"But you're dead," Mirrin whispered. He simply smiled – a familiar smile – and plunged the dagger into her heart.

It was nearing night fall. The patrols would be back from The City Square soon to continue their usual lives following the celebrations of Salvation Day. But still Neave waited. She remained squatting in the shadowed safety of the dark alleyway . She feared the surprise of veiled figures waiting in the shadows to ambush any returning Scholars and she could not face the uncertainty that lay beyond. However, she knew she had to make a decision before the patrols returned.

She poked her head around the alley entrance. The coast was clear. She took a deep breath and dashed across the street. There she ducked down under one of the window sills of the meeting place with her back pressed tight against the wall of the mansion. She again looked up and down the street. All was empty. Neave shook her head in an attempt to clear her thoughts and fears. She was on edge.

She tried to relax the tension in her shoulders and slowly, deliberately – aware of every slight sound she made – turned towards the window. The sill was level with her eyes. She breathed out slowly and wiped her sweaty hands on her shirt. Then she grabbed the window ledge.

The seconds ticked away as she strained to catch a sound from within. She imagined the worst coming for her through the dark gaping mouth that was the window, pulling her inside and swallowing her whole. *Is that someone breathing on my finger tips or just the draft?*

She let out the breath she had been holding and felt her hands beginning to go numb as she grasped the window ledge ever tighter in the biting cold of the evening air.

Once you have finished debating whether or not you will jump through this window, thought Neave to herself, *the sun will have set and you'll be dead in a mass grave.* Neave laughed nervously to herself and made a reckless decision.

She used all her might to heave herself through the window. She landed on the other side, crashing heavily, with a loud thump that disturbed the stillness of the place.

The stench of blood pervaded her nose. Neave almost jumped right back out, but managed to hold herself, pushed up against the underside of the window, every sense on high alert.

The room was dark, but the light entering through the window behind her was sufficient to make distinct the more prominent objects in the room; the toppled chairs and overturned cushions left by the running Gwakas. Her vision however, struggled in vain to reach the recesses of the chamber. Except one corner, where her attention was snagged by a flicker of light.

It was a flame, seemingly burning on the floor. Still crouching, Neave scuttled over to where it lay and almost laughed. She glanced over her shoulder at the ceiling and sure enough the chandelier had fallen and rolled into the corner. Now it deserved the name even less. The framework was misshapen, and its shielding was shattered.

She crouched down beside it and gently moved the shards of glass out of the way. The tiny flame wobbled dangerously, and Neave held her breath. The fire had been drowned with the wick soaked through with oil, but some still remained in the oil font.

It took several moments, but soon she had the lamp standing upright and the flame flickering enough to light the room. She held it above her head to illuminate her surroundings. She soon wished she hadn't. On the floor among a jumble of cushions lay a body.

Suddenly she despised that lantern, hated it with all her being. She flung it across the room where it hit the wall and shattered, extinguishing the flame.

Neave sank to the boards on her knees, face in her hands. There was a violent burning in her throat and her eyes stung. It was too much. She got her feet under her, blundered towards the window and managed to climb out, landing on the other side. She staggered on, moving towards The Outer City, fleeing the horror she had witnessed.

CHAPTER 4
Fire

A wind formed around the peak of a jagged mountain. It whistled through boulders and loose stones. Through a valley, it passed, fanning the scarce grass growing there. Beyond the mountain range it descended onto a city; it lost most of its ferocity and lazily breezed its way between shelters.

Soon the wind reached an old building, larger than many of its neighbours. It drifted through the windows and creaking doors that were flung open, gaping as if to swallow the night. It sailed around a bend and continued along until it gently ruffled the hair of an otherwise unmoving body lying on the wooden floor.

The wind crusted the blood that pooled around the body. It sensed something there. It rattled against bone, searching. The wind spun around in circles and then dived. It found its way down and twined around muscle and sinew, beating its way through the bars and freeing the spirit imprisoned there.

Then the wind proceeded on out a window and through the night continuing beyond Thamisveil. Here it encountered a coastal wind far stronger.

Neave continued running away from the harrowing events of the night. Try as she might, she could not keep the nightmare visions from forming in her mind's eye. She couldn't expunge the image of her mother's beautiful face framed by her own blood; her lifeless eyes staring straight through her. The deep red syrup was everywhere. Matted into her hair, leaking from the corner of her mouth and dried into the creases of her hands. Her life was trickling from her breast, dripping to the floor like a leaky tap.

Neave imagined her mother lying there – side pierced by a spear – calling out for help and a faceless raider finding her instead and stabbing her in the chest. It would have been easier than taking her captive and carrying her away injured.

Neave heard voices ahead. She was now walking, trying to blink away tears. She was very tired. But she could not stop. If she did, she knew she would breakdown. A sob raked through her body and her legs shook uncontrollably. *How could this have happened? How did my mother meet the same fate as my father? Will her soul make the death journey? Or will she be forever wandering; crying out eternally for help that will never come?* Without a death ceremony Neave thought it very likely. She could not bear it, both her parents. What would become of her? Was it her destiny to follow them; to never find rest?

A wind blew up from the south, smelling slightly of salt. It whipped her hair wildly around her head and cooled her sweaty, burning face. It pushed at her as if urging her onwards or perhaps warning her?

Something was wrong. Neave stopped abruptly. She now not only heard the voices, she saw their origin too. In between the trees in front of her, Neave saw flames. She crept closer, keeping to the shadows of the bushes and relying on the night to veil her from their view. She peaked around a shrub and a horrible spectacle met her eyes.

It was a spacious clearing and the captors had made use of it. Three fires formed a circle, of sorts. They lit up the front row of trees and cast the rest into greater shadow.

In the centre of this ominous circle of light sat a group of Gwakas. There were a handful of them, back to back with wrists and ankles tied. Their necks were fastened together with rope that was, in turn, fixed to a stake protruding from the very centre of the circle.

The fettered Gwakas were not strangers to Neave. Facing her was Linken. His usually bright, amiable face was contorted with fear and his bruised, dirty features streaked with tears. Tied to him were others from the mansion where the Scholars had held their meeting. Neave had to stop herself from hurrying to them. She realised she'd be no help to her friends tied up alongside them.

The captors sat around fires cooking mountain rabbits on spits. All wore veils shrouding their heads that only revealed their eyes. Everyone was still. They did not speak to one another and ate in silence.

Who are these captors? The government's minions? No, that makes no sense. Why would they come out here with the captives and not just execute them in the city like so many others.

Presently another Gwaka entered the clearing. All sitting Gwakas came to their feet immediately.

That must be the leader of the gang.

"Are all the prisoners still here? No troubles I hope?" The newcomer asked, looking towards a Gwaka to his right. Neave presumed he had been left in charge while the leader was away.

"None at all sir, none at all." He said, stepping forward and swelling up in pride. "Such a thing would never–"

He cut off as the leader waved his hand for silence. "I wish not to listen to your endless chatter. Have you some food prepared for my return?"

The Gwaka, visibly deflated, muttered something Neave did not quite catch. He then hurried over to a cook fire to cut some of the rabbit meat himself.

Neave pulled her attention away from him and back to the leader. He was speaking again. "The Shadow Master has ordered that we take the prisoners directly to Itzal Mal. He desires more Servants and believes we have captured sufficient rebels to keep them in check for a while. The Shadow Master has also commanded that some Servants go back to the city to keep the government in order. The rest will continue with me and the prisoners to Itzal Mal."

Neave's thoughts began to wander as the leader started calling forth Gwakas to return to the city at dawn. Her mind was racing. Then realisation flooded her entire being.

It's the attacker with the spear I glimpsed in the mad rush to escape these same assailants. The pieces are starting to fit together. This so-called Shadow Master has sent out his servants to raid the Scholars and frighten the rebels from their cause.

Neave did not like where her thoughts were leading. It meant a traitor in their midst. *But what can I do?* Neave knew the answer to this too. *Nothing, at least not by myself.*

Neave backed away, not making a sound as she moved through the trees. When she was out of earshot she started to run. Once she knew she was a safe distance from the fires she stumbled to the ground and could not bring herself to rise. Her legs shook with exertion and warm tears spilt over her flushed cheeks.

First father and mother and now Linken and the others.

They were not dead yet, but Neave did not think they would be alive for much longer unless they became servants to this Shadow Master.

She curled up until her forehead rested on her knees. She rocked back and forth and thought about her parents. She had always refused to remember her father to protect herself from what remembering would bring with it. She would never forget her mother; her steely determination and rock-hard strength. Her never-ending courage that had kept Neave moving forward even in the most difficult of times.

A cool breeze grabbed at her hair and toyed with the frayed ends of her ripped trousers. Neave had not noticed the rents. Her mother had repaired them for her just last week.

"But why?" Neave asked of the air. "Why does it have to be this way?"

"Why did they have to die?" A small voice asked back, suddenly. The voice was rich and filled Neave with a sense of strength and certainty. It seemed to come from the wind itself.

"Yes, I want to know" Neave said pleadingly. "Tell me why?"

"Maybe," the small voice answered, "maybe it's because they were important."

Neave sat up. "You mean they were rebels?" Neave did not expect a reply and did not need one. She already knew the answer. "Murdered," Neave whispered to herself. "It has a name.

Murder!" She was on her feet now and shouting. "They were martyrs," she screamed at the heavens. She now knew who to blame for their deaths. For her life. For everything. Neave had admired her mother's strength. Had relied on it. Her mother was gone now, and she had to take it up herself. She turned towards the mountain and looked up at its menacing peak; dark even against the night sky. The sides of her mouth curled, and her nose wrinkled up and met her frowning brows to form a vicious snarl. Any who had the misfortune to look upon her in this moment, would not for an instant have doubted that she promised a terrible death to those who had destroyed her life.

She ran on into the night. Not towards Itzal Mal but back in the direction of Thamisveil. Alone, she knew she could not help these poor captive Gwakas or get her revenge, so she decided to regroup and seek allies for her cause.

CHAPTER 5
Cheese Grater

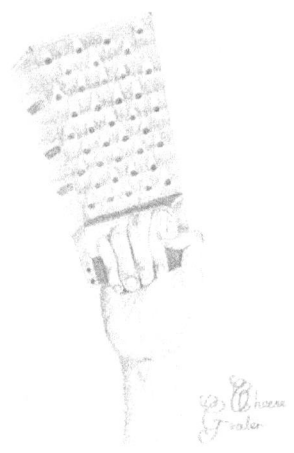

As Neave drank her tea, its familiar taste warmed her soul. The drink itself, by any standard of objectivity, was terrible. It was hard to come by fresh herbs and hot water was out of the question, but it reminded her of home.

She sat in Lewellyn's kitchen looking at him over the tea pot. His house was grimy and only had one room, but he was better off than most of those enduring the conditions of The Outer City.

Neave had gambled with her life by returning to the city and knocking on Lewellyn's door. The patrols were on high alert after the events of Salvation Day. She had crept up through the alleys behind Lewellyn's house and tapped lightly on the door. She had then melted back into the shadows of the neighbouring houses and waited. So, when a terrified Lewellyn poked his head around the door, Neave had been overjoyed.

Lewellyn cleared his throat and Neave jumped and shook herself back into the present. She was very tired, but she needed to offload the events of the day.

"I need...I need to tell you something." Neave struggled for a moment, rubbed her forehead and wiped a hand over her eyes.

"Maybe it is a better idea to go lie down and rest a while?" Lewellyn suggested gently.

Neave shook her head. "No, no! I need to tell you what I saw."

She lifted her chipped teacup with two shaking hands, sipped and began to talk. "I found my mother's dead body. I found it in the house after you had promised to find her and come back for me." Lewellyn was crying, but Neave could not bring herself to care, she was too tired. She continued, telling of her escape out of the city and how she stumbled across the group of captives held by strange veiled Gwakas.

"There is another force at work that we do not know of. Those who captured some of our Scholars named him Shadow Master. I gathered no useful information, but I believe that this dark force is manipulating our government."

Lewellyn stared at her in amazement. Then quickly buried his face in his tea, trying to cover his disbelief.

"Please Lewellyn, believe me. This is bigger than we thought, and I need answers. The only one I know able to tell me is far away and I will need the strength of all the Scholars to face what might come at us. I am not leaving Linken and the others to their deaths."

Neave breathed out heavily and loosened her strangling grip on the cup handle. Lewellyn was nodding. She had convinced him. "We will have to smuggle a large number of Gwakas out of the city. It is not the same as a lone Gwaka by the cover of dark," replied Lewellyn.

"We need a plan," said Neave. She was so tired, but this had to be done before she could rest.
Lewellyn's face adopted a grim expression, but all he said was,

"May we all come out of this alive. I'll put the kettle on."

Neave squatted in the alleyway exactly where she had the previous afternoon. Directly in front of her was another passageway and to her right the rich merchant house, its vacant eyes swallowing up the early dawn light. This place now held too many dark memories. They oppressed the very air she breathed, weighing it down until Neave felt the pressure of it pulling at her shoulders. Strongest of all was the memory of her mother's empty, staring eyes. Her body had most likely been removed; carted to one of the mass graves in the south. Mysterious deaths or disappearances were not considered a big deal and nothing was ever done about them. Thinking about it now Neave was able to see, with a fresh understanding, the strangeness of this. Was this another effect of the Shadow Master controlling the government's actions? Hopefully they would find answers to these questions soon enough, if they managed to escape Thamisveil alive.

Lingering on such memories was dangerous. Neave knew this from the experience of her father's disappearance. She pushed the thoughts aside and the pressure lessened slightly. She had not wished to return here but had finally agreed to Lewellyn's plan. It made sense, though it tore at her. The house met their needs perfectly. Neave had seen the previous owner chained to Linken; captured with the others – meaning the house should be deserted for a long time yet, giving sufficient time for them to achieve what they needed to and be on their way before anyone was any the wiser. At least, Neave hoped.

Lewellyn and Neave had discussed strategies in his kitchen over more cups of tea until Neave's eyes drooped to the point where she stared through slits, and the candlelight burned into her brain so that it felt as if a labourer group was pick-axing trenches in her head. At this point Lewellyn had stood and declared that they had planned enough, and it was time for him to inform the Scholars that they were gathering.

Neave had been far too exhausted to protest and the last thing she remembered was Lewellyn gathering his cloak and readying himself to leave. Then her head had slipped from her hands and her cheek hit the table.

The next thing she knew, Lewellyn was shaking her shoulder vigorously and speaking in her ear.

"Neave, wake up! It's time to leave."

She had jerked and come back to consciousness. They had quickly wolfed down a scrap of breakfast while dawn was yet far off and had then set out at a brisk pace to the merchant house.

And here they were, all the Scholars that lived on the south side of the city, split into two groups led by Neave and Lewellyn. Neave could see Lewellyn peering anxiously out from an opposite alley way.

They had devised a plan and Lewellyn had sent its design to the Scholars that lived in The High End.

Neave glanced over her shoulder at her group of rebels. They were ragged, but large enough in number for their purpose – a dozen, rags hanging off their shoulders and a jumble of weaponry, ranging from lengths of iron or wood, to kitchen utensils. Neave caught sight of a middle aged Gwaka holding a cheese grater. This could turn nasty. They had to be quick.

Neave peered around the corner of the building again and instantly jerked her head back. They had timed it well. A group of soldiers escorting labourers was heading in their direction. She lifted her eyes to meet the gaze of Lewellyn opposite her, nodded once and thrust her clenched fist into the air, the gesture they had agreed upon to indicate readiness and silence. There was a whisper of weapons being drawn or lowered and ropes being adjusted. Into the stillness that followed, Neave could clearly define the soldiers' crunch of boots on the dirt road and the hesitant shuffle of the labourers' bare feet.

According to plan, Neave dashed out of cover and headed straight for the lead soldier. She sensed the members of her group spreading out behind her and to either side just before she collided with her opponent. She saw the startled expression on his face as her fist smashed into his collarbone. He went down with a cry of pain. So did the next one, crumpling around his broken ribs. She pushed on, passed fighting pairs until she confronted a frightened face, crouching down in the churned-up dirt, arms over his head. His feet were bare, and his poor state marked him a labourer. She loathed to be rough to those who already had so much violence in their lives, but it was necessary. Neave unwound the rope from around her waist and quickly proceeded to tie the wretches' hands and feet. Then she ripped a piece of fabric from the Gwaka's hem and used it to gag his whimpers.

Neave took up her staff and spun upright to join the fray again. "Neave! Behind you."

Neave ducked and rolled to the side. A knife whistled through the air where her head had been just moments before. She turned on her back and watched as her attacker advanced on her. She had rolled badly, landing on her staff; she would have no time to retrieve it from under her to defend herself. She would have to dart in quickly, past his knife to hit something vital. Neave's fear crept through her stomach and constricted her throat. She cast around for another option. She needed something. A leverage.

The soldier stepped up to her. She had no other choice. Neave tensed her muscles ready to leap from her crouched over position. The Gwaka raised his knife just as a stick flew through the air and struck him in the stomach.

Neave sat in the muck of the street, stunned. Then she turned her head to follow the path of the flying stick, back to the Gwaka who had thrown it. The Gwaka stood, concentration still written on her face, but unaware of the soldier creeping up behind her, spear raised.

Neave reached out a hand towards her and opened her mouth as if to utter a warning. But it was too late. The Gwaka's chest split, and a glitter of metal pierced through her shirt front. An expression of shock spread through her face as she looked down at her breast. Then she jerked, as if attempting to escape her inevitable fate. She composed herself, summoned her strength, drew the knife that hung at her belt and flipped it back to stab her murderer in the eye. The instant before she fell, she fixed her eyes straight at Neave.

Neave could not have broken that stare if she had wanted to. That gaze revealed the Gwaka's mind to Neave. Anger, determination and a belief that Neave could not quite understand. It dug deep into Neave's soul, coursed through her being and brought to the surface all the fury that had been bottled up. That stare cried out for retribution, for justice, for freedom.

Neave placed a hand over her heart, saluting the Gwaka's soul as her body fell to the ground, then turned her head to face the soldier who was recovering with gasping breaths and holding his stomach. He was winded and blood stained the cloth in between his fingers. The stick must have punctured skin. The female Gwaka had had a strong, accurate arm.

Neave smiled and slowly climbed to her feet. She had not even known the Gwaka, yet she had sacrificed her life for Neave. She felt she owed her something. Her smile faded and a snarl took its place. She would take up the Gwaka's dying wish.

Neave let out a vicious cry of anger and ran at the soldier, lifting her staff over her head. He had no chance against Neave's wrath. She was a tempest, merciless; proceeding with no remorse for the damage she would do. As the soldier struggled to straighten with knife in hand against the pain of his stomach, Neave brought her staff down on his head. There was a crack of splintering bone and the Gwaka crumpled.

Neave looked about her, the winds of rage and bloodlust still seethed through her. She craved another opponent. But there were no more. Neave took a deep breath, calmed her racing heart, and the anger slowly dissipated within her. Her shoulders slumped and exhaustion hit her like a hammer. She looked around at her fellow Scholars. They were all breathing hard, many sported wounds, but she was emboldened to see no others, besides the Gwaka who had saved Neave's life, had died. That brought their number down to thirty, but they had done well. They had been quick, efficient.

A moan to her right caught her attention. The labourers were huddled together in the dirt. They had been useless to both sides during the exchange, chained together as they were, not even able to run away.

"Scholars we have work to do yet." Neave said as loudly as she dared.

Everyone commenced their task, stripping the soldiers' corpses of their uniforms, claiming their superior weapons and then dragging the bare bodies into the mansion. It was not a permanent solution, but hopefully the corpses were not discovered before the Scholars were far away.

A Gwaka handed Neave a bundle of clothing removed from the lead officer of the squad and the key to unlock the labourers' chains. She quickly pulled the officer's uniform on over her own apparel and walked over to the line of labourers.

They had been gagged and their hands bound. Five Scholars stood guard over them and they let her pass to unlock the first Gwaka. This was the one Neave had trussed up during the fight and his feet were still tied. His expression was mournful, and he did not acknowledge her in any way even when the ring unclipped from around his ankle.

Neave sighed. Most Gwakas had no spirit left and it saddened her to see it; she moved on to the next one.

She bent to undo the clasp. The band had only just sprung open, when he jumped to his feet and strove to dash away. One of Neave's rebels knocked him on the head with her club before he had ventured three paces, sending him unconscious to the ground. The other labourers cowered away from the scene which would hopefully prevent any other escape plans.

The labourers were then ushered into the mansion along with the dead soldiers. Their feet were bound with rope to prevent escape. The unconscious Gwaka was dragged in after them.

Neave proceeded to lock the chains around those rebels left with no uniforms. Soon a dozen of her Scholars stood in a labourer line and the remaining eight surrounded them all dressed in the soldiers' uniforms. Neave was the last to join the procession. On the way she scooped up the officer's whip. She looked over the street one last time. No one had appeared yet and only a patch of churned up dirt suggested that anything unusual had occurred.

Neave nodded to the Gwakas behind her and they began to march out of the city. For retribution, for justice, for freedom.

THE SHADOW MASTER'S EYE

CHAPTER 6
Sage Gwaka

Sage Gwaka

Neave crested a hill, marching before the other south force Scholars, and there it was: the valley that would hopefully hold the answers.

Neave gazed down at Minethresan Valley, diminished from years of neglect and the rule of Itzal Mal, but nevertheless one of the most beautiful scenes Neave had ever looked upon.

A tiny trickle of fresh water cut the valley in two. The grass was in the late stages of decay and steep, cracked cliffs halfway through the valley spoke of a long-forgotten waterfall.

She stepped forward into the valley and shivered though it was not cold. Indeed, heat flooded her, but the warmth was quashed by a gloomy darkness. Neave groped after it, trying to recover even a single ember of warmth when suddenly, before her eyes, she encountered a utopian vision, a miracle.

A fierce river surged through the valley on a natural course; around boulders, through tall grasses, thundering into a waterfall and finally gathering in huge lakes at the base of the valley. And there were human children (who, to Neave, looked like little, handsome Gods), running through the knee length grass and splashing in the shallows of the mighty river.

This can't be real, thought Neave, and she shook her head, in an attempt to keep a grasp on reality.

She took a single step forward and the magnificent river and dancing children dissolved in Neave's mind's eye and she could again only see the small trickle of water running down sloping hills and past sad, nodding reeds.

Her heart sank. For a moment she had lived in the vision and her soul had lifted with the sound of the children's play. She felt an overwhelming sensation of longing for what she had experienced; she desperately wanted to be one of those children. But reality was once more staring her in the face; the Shadow Master's touch on the earth again spread as far as the eye could see.

She peered back at her company and was horrified to witness that those in front were standing stock still, staring into the distance with expressions of awe on their faces. As Neave watched, some recovered themselves and stumbled forward into the valley. Many looked around in confusion and some sadness. They were all snared in the same vision.

As the Scholars one by one stumbled into the valley, they gathered around her as if she were a protective shield against the prevailing evil. She needed Lewellyn. Deep down Neave still felt that, besides her mother, Lewellyn was the only one able to help when a problem arose. The throng crowded around her, murmuring and buzzing about the curious things they had all witnessed.

She scanned the scene to find Lewellyn and saw him waving his arms about in a ridiculous fashion.

Neave could feel the frustration building in her chest. "Shut up all of you, let me through!" she screamed. A hush fell over the group and they started making way for their leader. As soon as there was an opening, Neave moved to meet Lewellyn. He was standing before a Gwaka and looking into his eyes. Neave approached him hesitantly.

"There is no recognition in his eyes," said Lewellyn without turning around. "They are as blank as glass."

Neave peered past his shoulder and understood what he meant. The Gwaka's eyes were black holes. He neither blinked nor twitched a muscle and, as she widened her gaze, Neave saw more of these Gwakas frozen in wonder, all standing in a line on the verge of entering the valley.

"What has happened to them?" Neave asked in horror. "They seem as if caught within the moment."

"Their bodies could be," replied Lewellyn.

"But what..." she trailed off as comprehension struck her. "Their souls have entered that utopian vision we saw?"

Lewellyn nodded his head. Neave felt sick. She reached out and touched the Gwaka's cheek and immediately wished she hadn't. It was icy cold and hard as rock. *Is he now made of stone?* she thought. *Is there anything in that body or is he just an empty husk? And what of his soul? Is it trapped in a fantasy; a vision of something all but erased from the memory of the world?*

Neave turned away feeling nauseous and spoke to the whole rebel group who were all staring up at her expectant and anxious.

"These Gwakas had good souls. And although those souls have been netted in an unreality, they were no less kind or brave than the rest of us. For they now face a hurdle that we may never know. They knew this journey would be fraught with danger, yet they continued on without a backward glance. They believed in the cause and I mourn each one of them."

The Scholars muttered in agreement and some wiped their eyes. The friends of those Gwakas openly wept.

"But now we must move on," exclaimed Neave. "The north group should already be waiting for us, and we have those who would kill us on our tails. There is no time to rest."

Later, Lewellyn and Neave stood outside the council tent in Minethresan valley. They had met the north group who had arrived not long before them and set up a rough camp with whatever they had been able to smuggle out of Thamisveil, including a tent.

The north band had ambushed a labourer line, stealing their buckets and wheelbarrows. They had packed them full of food and blankets. All the other council members had been part of the north band and Neave was not surprised to find out Morgan had brought along the tent. She was not one to miss an opportunity for comfort, even when thrift and prudence were necessary.

"There is no way you will not be chosen," said Lewellyn. "Everyone has seen what you have done, and they have nowhere else to turn. This is a council meeting and they are here to judge you. My advice is to tread carefully, as you are not yet a council member ."

Lewellyn clapped Neave on the shoulder, smiled reassuringly and entered Morgan's tent, where the council meeting was taking place. Neave followed in his wake. She heard the tent flaps flutter shut behind her. The interior was badly lit with a single battered torch from a labourer line sitting on the floor in the middle, gently lighting the members' legs and casting their faces into shadow.

Lewellyn stood directly before her; to advance any further into the tent was impossible. The small space was crammed with the five Gwakas and the torch. There was a shuffle of feet as the council bunched together to let Neave wedge in next to Lewellyn.

"Now that we are all here we can begin. Kimberly?" This was said by a Gwaka to Neave's right, who's face carried a morose expression. Her name was Morgan.

Kimberly was an honest Gwaka with an open face that was fuller than most. She cleared her throat before speaking. "This gathering is to vote on a new leader and decide how and when we proceed. Neave has led us here for reasons unknown to me and I suppose most of us, and I believe I speak for everyone when I demand to know more."

Morgan spoke up, agreeing and adding: "I would like to hear from Neave herself why *she*," she emphasised the pronoun and looked pointedly at everyone except Neave, "marched us through the mountains."

Neave felt the resentment and hatred emitting from Morgan in waves that washed over her, turning her insides to ice. Neave got the impression that Morgan did not like the idea of someone younger than herself leading the cause.

Kimberly inclined her head, "Neave, if you would please?"

It wasn't really a question and Neave had no intention of challenging the council at this time, in this place. Everyone had a right to know what was driving them all on this desperate mission and so Neave told the tale of how she had stumbled across the Servants, discovered the Shadow Master and uncovered the truth of his manipulative power over the government.

"Overthrowing the government will only get us so far," Neave exclaimed. "The fundamental problems would still remain. The Shadow Master needs to be killed and we are the only Gwakas I know able to fight him. If he is not stopped, our lives will never improve, and he will eliminate the Scholars one by one. You were all there when the Servants attacked us. He knows of our organisation. He will hunt us down to the last and then there won't be anyone left to stand up to him."

"My mother did a good job gathering as many Scholars as she did, but she waited too long. There is a time for patience, and a time for action. The time for action is now. This is not a game where we dream of taking down the government and rise up victorious to make a better life for everyone. This is life or death and I am not turning away from it. I will go whether you agree with me or not. In order to claim the retribution, justice and freedom we deserve, I am ready to face my death.

Kimberly stared at her open mouthed and Lewellyn discreetly patted Neave on the back while Morgan spluttered, then burst out, "She insults us." She pointed a finger at Neave's face, her eyes fire, "She insults us to our faces." She now openly glared at her and Neave bowed her head, remembering Lewellyn's advice.

Into this awkward silence came a cool voice. "This is of no relevance to our situation. Kimberly back to the point please."

Neave looked to a Gwaka on Lewellyn's left. Delyssius had stern features that seemed set in stone. Her eyes were grey and her lips thin.

Kimberly inclined her head again and smoothed down her shirt, "Yes, well, we need to vote on a new leader."

"I do not consider this a question at all. Is it not obvious?" stated Delyssius. Neave had not heard her speak very often, but when she did it was in a controlled voice that never seemed to waver.

She looked to Neave with her calm gaze. "Who was the one to discover this Shadow Master? Who was the one to smuggle us out of the city? You heard her speak. She is her mother's daughter."

"No!" The word burst out of Morgan at the suggestion. She seemed to realise that she had taken it too far, and softened her tone, "She is too young, merely a child, too inexperienced."

"If you believe she is a child, you have no sense." Delyssius interceded, "She has done more than any one of us. She's wise beyond her years and has shown her skill and passion in many areas. Neave is the one to lead us. She will go whether we like it or not and she needs us to have her back."

"If she goes or not is not the point in question." Morgan insisted with a look of frustration on her face. "She can still go under another's leadership."

"And who would you suggest in her place?" responded Kimberly .

Morgan looked at them stubbornly, "Well, someone older and more experienced in these matters. All in this tent have been with the Scholars longer than Neave."

"How long you have been with the Scholars is absolutely irrelevant. Neave has the vision to lead and the Scholars trust her."

"She is too young and –."

"Time is of the essence", Delyssius interrupted her yet again, as calmly as before, "and we must vote. I nominate Neave for our new leader. Who here agrees?"

She stared around the tent, demanding an answer from everyone. All nodded except for Morgan who crossed her arms and scowled. "You mark my words and think back to what I said when we are all rotting with crows pecking at our eyes. From what I understand, she plans to come up against this Master of Shadows. You shall all see how that ends for us."

"Neave," said Kimberly, ignoring Morgan, "are you willing to take on the role of leader of this Scholar organisation? Will you listen to the advice of the council and your Scholars and treat them fairly and with kindness?"

"I am and I will." Neave replied with no hesitation.

"Then it is decided." Kimberly continued, "Neave is to carry on in Mirrin's footsteps and be our new leader."

Delyssius nodded, "I will announce it to the Scholars."

She exited with a shuffle of bodies that made the stakes of the tent groan. Neave watched as the flaps fluttered shut and was not sure what to think. She was now the official leader of the Scholars and yet, everything had transpired so quickly. Neave was still coming to terms with the fact that she had taken control of the south group and organised the escape for the whole Scholar organisation. It had happened so naturally and now they were here, with her as leader of the Scholars, about to run headlong towards victory or a gruesome death.

The Scholars gathered, waiting in apprehension. Their new leader was chosen and about to be presented to them. The haze of excitement hovering over the crowd was almost visible. They watched the hill outside the council tent waiting for a figure to emerge.

Neave climbed the short hill before the meeting tent. Her nerves jangled as she slowly stepped up the slope. Delyssius had announced her before all the Scholars. Neave was leader. There was no doubt about it now.

She took one more step and crested the hill. Below her the Scholars stared up to meet her gaze. Neave grinned broadly and threw her fist into the air. The Gwakas stamped their feet and shouted with abandon. At least, that is what an outsider may have thought. To Neave it was a cry of hope.

Neave walked down the hill and was engulfed in a swarm of Gwakas slapping her on the back and offering her congratulations. She smiled, accepting praise, but it was with reservation. She had a task to complete. She had information to gather.

Neave nodded to the Gwakas close to her and started to move away from the group. It took several minutes to be free of the crowd. She searched for a place where she would be visible to all. There was a large stone to her right. She climbed atop it.

She waved the crowd to silence, "For a long time now we have believed that the government was the cause of all of our pain. We have all experienced the consequences of living under our government in some form, whether through the death of one close or by having to endure the harsh conditions of the slums and starvation. For a long time we have thought that overthrowing the government was the answer to our problems. Our purpose was to replace it with something better. But now we know the true force at work."

A whisper of agitation passed through the gathered listeners as they digested this new and alarming information.

"Before we came here, I overheard the Servants, as they call themselves, conversing about a Shadow Master. He is their lord and is the one who has been controlling the government." A wave of horror swept through the Scholars at this statement. "The Shadow Master is the puppeteer pulling all the strings. He is the one to blame for our miserable existence." The crowd stirred again.

"He must be eliminated if we are to ever have peace again!" The Scholars roared. Neave gestured at the valley around them and continued. "We came here to find answers about the Shadow Master. You all know the myths of Sage Gwaka, the wisest of all Gwakas. My mother came here twenty years ago searching for answers to her own questions. Now I invite you all to join me in our endeavour to find the truth."

Neave walked along the bank of the once magnificent river, its bed now overgrown with weeds. Following close behind were the other Scholars. She felt the presence of Sage Gwaka up ahead. He seemed to urge her towards him. Presently she caught sight of him facing eastward toward the rocky slopes of the forgotten waterfall. He was crouching on a tree stump with his hands clasped before him.

Neave glanced behind her and waved the awestruck Scholars onward. She had found him where her mother had discovered him so long ago. Neave stepped cautiously closer until she stood right before him. He did not twitch an eyelid.

Neave could see he was an incredible age. The myths spoke of him having lived for hundreds of years and Neave now believed them. His hands were knobbly and his face was weathered to the point where parts of his flesh seemed eroded away. He wore no clothing and his skin had a decidedly grey tone to it, barely covering his bones.

Sage Gwaka did not look up or make any outward sign that he had perceived their presence, instead he kept his eyes fixed on the ground before him.

"Wise Sage Gwaka?" said Neave. He made no response but to rock back and forth on his log slightly. Neave cleared her throat and tried again, aware of the others standing behind her. "Please, Sage Gwaka, we have some questions we had hoped you might answer?" He remained silent.

Neave was beginning to lose hope that he would ever reply. *Why is he not speaking? Mother had a whole conversation with him, but then why had he not told her back then about the Shadow Master?* Neave's questions were multiplying in her head at breakneck speed. They had come all this way, endured so much to find Sage Gwaka, and he just rocked back and forth on his log. But there was something peaceful and calming about that rocking. So gentle and rhythmic. *Wouldn't it be nice,* thought Neave, *to sit, not a care in the world, let it all go, and simply sway and reflect on life, past and coming.*

Neave pulled away from her daydream and snapped back to reality, only to realise she was sitting down in the dirt facing Sage Gwaka. She hurriedly jumped upright as if stung on the backside by a bee. She refused to look behind her, at the others. She was becoming confused and annoyed.

Then she distinctly saw a tremor run through Sage Gwaka's body. She stepped forward, suddenly anxious for the frail looking Gwaka, then immediately lost all sympathy as she realised he was laughing. Out of the deepest recesses of his body came a warm chuckle that vibrated his being and peaked her fury.

"Good, good. So young, so determined. You must learn calmness. You rush hither and thither always so hurried, no time to be centred. You did well young one, to break the trance as you did and you will need that determination, that sense of need if you are to face the Shadow Master."

Neave stared at him open mouthed, not certain how to respond, his voice was so soft, yet carried such weight of wisdom and certitude.

"That is what you came here for, is it not? To learn about the Shadow Master?"

Now Neave did look back at her company. They all seemed just as taken aback as she, though Delyssius did give her a small nod. Neave turned back, "Yes, that is why we are here."

Sage Gwaka gave no response and Neave let out a frustrated sigh, not caring anymore how she appeared to the Scholars.

"We would like to know," she said slowly and clearly, carefully articulating each word so that she could not be misunderstood and holding her frustration in her clenched fists, "what the Servants are, where the Shadow Master is and what exactly he is."

Sage Gwaka nodded his head, acknowledging the questions. He did not answer straight away. Neave was beginning to realise that haste was not his modus operandi. She took some deep breaths, to steady herself and waited.

"The Servants are Gwakas," eventually came the response, "captured from communities like yours and forced against their will to serve the Shadow Master. They do his bidding and are so completely under his control that they would not hesitate to kill themselves if he ordered. Most are captured as children and raised to be Servants. They know only the Shadow Master and do nothing but serve him."

There was another long pause before Sage Gwaka spoke again. "As for your other questions; Uzma, the Shadow Master, is one of the last existing humans, though he no longer deserves the name. His body is ruined, and he is no longer capable of empathy for another being. He would wipe out your entire city without a second thought for those who would suffer, if he did not need you to provide him with servants and his servants with food."

"The tyrant lives in a dark cavern towards that peak." And, without taking his eyes off the dirt before him, he pointed north towards Itzal Mal.

CHAPTER 7
Itzal Mal

Minethresan Valley was now long behind the Scholars and a grey expanse of rock lay before them. Above rose the ominous mountain, overshadowing them, and blocking out the sky. The nearing night fall cast shadows that leaked into the world too quickly .

Neave swept her gaze behind her to see the extended line of Scholars marching through the stone landscape. They had been on the march since daybreak on the morning after they had spoken to Sage Gwaka.

Neave heard a rattle of rocks skidding on rocks, announcing the presence of an approaching individual from the north. It was a scout she'd sent out earlier. He stood next to Neave and spoke calmly. "There is a good campsite ahead, a hollow between large boulders protected against the wind, Neave Gwaka."

He gave a slight bow and Neave inclined her head to indicate she had understood. The scout ran on ahead again to ensure the path was clear as Neave stood and waited for Delyssius to come alongside her. "We will be stopping for the night in a hollow up ahead. Could you pass on the message to the other council members please?"

Delyssius nodded and obliged, turning to the Gwaka behind her and conveying the news. Neave left her to it and continued on, winding her way through the treacherous footing on the unstable, loose stones that slipped under foot. The gathering dark made it harder to navigate and increasingly dangerous to walk through. *It's a good time to stop for the night*, thought Neave.

A face appeared around the corner of a large bolder to Neave's left. The scout beckoned to her and she picked her way to him. Behind the rock lay a glade of stone.

The Gwakas set up camp. This didn't take long, as they dared not light fires for fear of attracting attention. Neave was handed some of the dried food from their supplies and laid down with her blanket to rest. Most everyone did the same, with the exception of the few assigned sentry duties.

It wasn't long before night had fully descended, and all was silent. Only the screech of an occasional crow disturbed the still air, yet Neave was restless. She could not settle under her blanket. The presence of the mountain seemed to be all around her, its shadow casting a feeling of foreboding over her. She rolled over again, twisting the blanket around herself even more. But it was no use. She couldn't sleep. She had to get up and do something.

Neave untangled herself from the blanket and let it fall to the ground. All around her the Scholars lay on the stone floor of the hollow and slept. She began to pick her way around them. Some stirred and muttered in their sleep as she passed.

They were her Scholars now . Her responsibility . She wondered if her mother had felt the same pressure of obligation and burden of duty for them. Mirrin had always seemed to know what to do. She had never questioned her actions for more than a second. Her stride had only faltered once – at Aieron's passing. But even then she had stayed strong for Neave and the Scholars. Aieron's disappearance had never weakened her resolve; on the contrary, it had strengthened her will to live and see those in power defeated. Mirrin would never experience their retribution, but Neave could finish the work her mother had started.

She was nearing the edge of the campsite now when something moving in the shadows caught her attention. As she focused her gaze she saw the feet, then the legs and torso of a standing Servant of the Shadow Master. His hand was clamped over Morgan's mouth, who was hanging stock still, with her toes only just brushing the stone floor; held up in the Gwaka's grip. In the other hand he held a knife, the blade pressed up against Morgan's throat. Neave's eyes travelled a little higher and met the Servants gaze through the slits of a veil.

Neave froze as memories flashed through her: the veiled figure drawing back his arm with a spear clutched in his hand. Her mother lying dead with a spear through her stomach.

This all flashed across her mind's eye as she watched on helplessly while the Servant drew his knife across Morgan's neck, dropped her in a heap and melted back into the shadows of a boulder. Neave tried to shout, but her throat was constricted with fear. As she stood, with strange croaking noises emanating from her mouth, she saw out of the corner of her eye, a movement in the shadows of another boulder. This time she did yell.

"Intruders! Servants in the camp!"

Several things occurred at once. The Scholars all woke in an instant and were up, holding weapons they had slept with and out of the shadows all around the camp came veiled Gwakas grasping spears. Someone grabbed Neave from behind and dragged her quickly backwards.

Neave struggled, trying to regain her feet and flailed behind her with her fists. There was a hollow thud and a low grunt from the Gwaka holding her shirt as one of her punches made contact.

"Neave, it's me." Lewellyn's voice reached her ears through the chaos that broke forth in the hollow. Neave was shocked to stillness and let him drag her back a few steps. She had been so certain that she was in the hands of a Servant and seconds from death.

"Are you going to help me and get up or am I to drag you all the way?"

Neave scrambled to her feet and ran with Lewellyn into the shadows and outside the campsite. She turned around to see groups of Scholars working to overcome the Servants. She longed to join them; to help her Scholars in any way she could.

Then suddenly it was all over. A dozen Servant bodies littered the ground and the ambush from the shadows ceased. Neave's breath came out in a rush and she could feel her muscles shaking from the sudden release of tension. It had all happened so suddenly and was over so quickly.

"That's it?" she asked of no one in particular.

Lewellyn had also halted and was staring around in some bewilderment.

"Is that all of them?" He similarly asked. "I thought it was an all-out attack."

A Gwaka approached Neave uncertainly and bowed her head,

"Neave Gwaka?"

"It's alright, you can speak," she said gently.

"I have the death toll if you would?"

Neave nodded, indicating for her to continue.

"Five of our Scholars and twelve Servants, Neave Gwaka. It seems as if this was a suicide mission. If you had not warned us, Neave Gwaka, they may have wiped us out."

"Thank you, ah—"

"My name is Pip." She smiled up at Neave. She was very young and eager and trusted completely that Neave could protect her .

"Thank you Pip. You have a difficult job and I appreciate what you do."

"Yes Neave Gwaka." She then scampered away.

Neave looked after her sadly, but when she turned back to Lewellyn her expression was fierce, "He must die, and I will not rest until the deed is done."

Lewellyn stepped back from the ferocity in her tone and face. *Good.* She thought with satisfaction and turned to the Scholars who were still recovering from the lightning flash fight with the Servants.

"Scouts, search the area for more of these creeping rats. We are breaking camp."

It was well into the afternoon and they had been hiking over an endless stretch of grey stone for hours, yet the sky was dark. Neave craned her neck to see the swirling, black clouds above them and just below, Itzal Mal's jagged peak clawing at the boiling thunder heads.

They were on the mountain's slopes now and their path had become decidedly steeper and more treacherous. The threat of miss-stepping and tumbling down the rocky slope was increasing, and some poor Scholars had already met their end in this gruesome fashion. Neave could remember the sight of the first victim's body lying disfigured at the base of the mountain. Yet this threat was dwarfed by the plaguing intruder creeping through the depths of their minds.

It was pervasive. Every Scholar was becoming increasingly affected by its crouching shadow. Neave had first become aware of the sensation as they had started their ascent of the mountain. It weighed heavy on her soul and seemed to set a large load on her shoulders. It was an intruder, ripping into her mind and sorting through her memories; casting out the good.

A scream sounded from behind and Neave spun around, fearing the worst. It was indeed grim, though not what Neave had expected to see. Down the line of Scholars following her, there was a disturbance. One had collapsed to his knees in the middle of the path with his hands over his head. He was muttering and moaning incoherently. As they watched, he began to bang his head on the stone before him. Again and again and again. Neave looked away, feeling the bile rise in her throat. She could not watch the torment.

Above, the peak of Itzal Mal rose. *This must be the work of the Shadow Master.* Neave would have bet her life on it.

Behind her the Gwaka screamed to the circulating clouds. "Too much. Too much!"

These were his final words, as he then keeled over and lay unmoving. There was only one thing she could do for this Scholar and that was to continue the upward trudge and take the life of the one to blame.

Neave could not remember anything of her past life. She could, however, feel. Though the memories were gone, the sensations of those moments remained. They piled on top of one another; anger, hatred, fear. Fear predominated, filling her soul with shivers that shook her body. She tried to push them away, restrain them from sweeping her over, but even the empty space that opened beyond, threatened to swallow all and send her into oblivion. She balanced as a tight rope walker does, a slight shift awry would find her tumbling into the abyss.

All the Scholars felt as though they stood on this knife's edge. More had collapsed, convulsing, before dropping lifeless to the ground from the tidal wave of feelings.

Neave had lost count of those who had died in their ascent but there was no time to mourn their loss. She only had one focus of thought now: The Shadow Master. She had to kill him. Neave could not recall why this was so important, but she knew it had to happen, and this overriding thought helped balance her mind and keep her emotions at bay. He had to die.

THE SHADOW MASTER'S EYE

CHAPTER 8
Bathamis

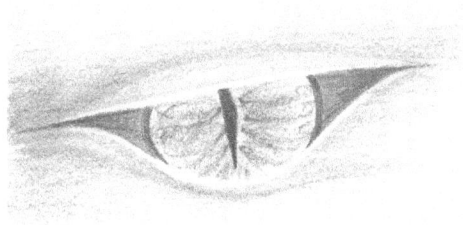

Neave took a step and hit flat rock. There was something strange about that, but she could not place it. Neave glanced up and saw a dark hole yawning widely in front of her; a cave. That meant something, but what exactly, she could not put her finger on. Then clarity of thought prevailed; "The Shadow Master," whispered Neave to herself.

Other Scholars began to join her on the plateau before the cave; only thirty or so had survived the journey, and all stared at the mouth of the cave. It was the entry to the home of the one who had made their life a misery for so long. Then, as if the Scholars were a single organism, everyone crept forward towards the cave. Their plan was simple and there was no need to review it. Neave waved them on. A gruesome stench met Neave's nose as she entered the cave entrance.

It took several moments for her eyes to adjust to the dim light of the cave. She held out her weapon; a spear retrieved from a dead Servant. *A whole lot of help this will be against attackers without my eyesight,* she thought to herself.

The cave began to form before her eyes. Neave would have screamed if she were not shaking so hard from fear. The walls of the room were lined with Servants holding double pointed spears. Their faces were obscured by veils, but their eyes glinted with malice.

However, the focal point of this frightening scene sat against the back wall on an iron throne. Neave's eyes strained to define him. He towered above her with a viciously barbed spear in his hand. His skin was grey, mottled black and rotting. It emanated the stench Neave had first encountered on entering the cave and stretched over thin, pale lips as he smiled. Yet none of this could compete with the monstrosity that sat in his eye socket.

It glowed and shimmered yellow; swirled and sucked the joy from life, consuming and pooling it in its inner depths. Neave was mesmerised by it and terrified of its radiating power. She saw The Shadow Master's lips twitch as if to smile wider.

To the left of The Shadow Master, Neave caught sight of a cage. As she strained her eyes to look closer she made out bony fingers gripping the bars. As her gaze moved from the hands up to meet the eyes of their owner, her heart sank and seemed to stop beating. Linken was staring back at her, with a look of despair painted across his corpselike face. This further steeled Neave's resolve and both her fists clenched tight as her attention returned to Uzma.

"Neave, welcome." He raised his head and laughed as the Servants lining the walls attacked.

Neave had no choice but to trust her Scholars to deal with the Servants; she had a job to do. She advanced several steps towards Uzma.

"Aieron!" The Shadow Master roared, spittle flying from his thin, grey lips, "come and join me."

While The Shadow Master was distracted, she lunged forward, driving the spear towards his midriff (The Shadow Master would be as dead as any other Gwaka if he copped a spear through his stomach). Swift as a snake striking for its prey, he rose, fending off her attack and sending her flying backwards. Neave hit the stone floor with a sickening crunch, knocking the wind out of her. She lay gasping, struggling to find breath enough to stand back up. *How could such a ravaged body produce such strength and agility?*

When she had recovered enough to suck in a breath, she slowly climbed back to her feet. The Shadow Master was patting the head of a man who knelt beside him. The stranger's face was lacerated with a web of scars. They ruined the darkly handsome features that lay beneath. He had a strong jaw and heavy brows over light blue eyes. There was something familiar about those eyes. His nose had been broken several times and had healed badly. The Shadow Master had called him Aieron, and the truth suddenly dawned on Neave.

She gasped. How could this be. Her father was dead. But looking at that face beneath those scars there was no doubt he was related to her.

"You know who he is, don't you." This was not a question.

Neave made eye contact with Uzma but could not find the strength to respond. Something of her fear must have shown on her face, for The Shadow Master smiled in satisfaction and both his eyes glinted with a fearsome light.

"How?" Neave managed to choke out.

The Shadow Master's smile grew even more malevolent. "I've known about your organisation for a long time. Aieron was a spy that I placed in your city to infiltrate the government, help filter out those who opposed it, feed me information. Aieron met your mother, who just happened to be the leader of the very organisation I was looking for. Imagine how pleased I was with him. Not only had he found the rebels but had also wormed his way into their ranks through the leader's affection."

He smiled dangerously down at Aieron.

"Then he deserted me." At these words The Shadow Master's face underwent an utter transformation. His features were suddenly horrifying to look upon. His anger so intense that Neave could almost feel heat radiating from him.

"After four years of no information, I was able to track him down and bring him back home. He is totally under my control now, aren't you my *dog*?" Aieron drew back from The Shadow Master as if he feared being slapped.

"The only reason I did not end his life as punishment for his treachery was because the affection he held with the rebel leader made him useful to me. I waited patiently, gathering information until it was the perfect time to strike. My pet was the one who killed your mother. Did you know that? Good doggy."

All the while a fearsome battle continued to rage between the scholars and the servants in the cave behind Neave. Lives were being lost on both sides.

Aieron looked up at his master, the lord of the world, and preened under his petting. He caught some of the conversation taking place between his master and the leader of the assailants. They were speaking about him. He smirked at how jealous the other servants would be. He would have to be cautious, some may attempt to kill him. He listened closer.

"Then he deserted me." The Shadow Master's voice was a growl and Aieron cowered at his feet, ashamed. *The Shadow Master can be very harsh*, thought Aieron. He remembered a time when he had even gone so far as to kill a servant as punishment for their disobedience.

The Shadow Master sneered down at Aieron. "You are totally under my control, aren't you my *dog*?" There seemed to be a threat in those words. Aieron hastily nodded his head vigorously to dispel any doubt of his loyalty, but a tiny voice in his mind reared up at the insult. He pushed the voice down. The Shadow Master had all but broken Aieron, to the point where his mind was no longer his own. But a remnant of his former self remained and occasionally crawled up out of the darkness to enter his consciousness. Why did this voice demand to be heard? He was dominated by The Shadow Master now and was better for it. Yet the voice grew ever louder.

Aieron considered the Gwaka facing The Shadow Master and the fog that clouded his view of the world lifted slightly. She reminded him of someone. A Gwaka he had once known. Someone precious.

He scrabbled through the fog in his mind, desperately trying to find a way out. Suddenly he burst free into what seemed to be sunlight. He looked back and saw the swirling mist behind him that ended quite abruptly and was suddenly assailed by memory.

He gasped in agony as again he lived the days of torture. The starvation. The loneliness. The harsh laughter and mockery of others as they watched his torment. And, of course, the pain. It was everywhere. Physical and psychological. The absolute terror that they may come for him again. The sleepless nights as a result of this. And there, at the heart of everything, was The Shadow Master, wielding a knife against him, amused by his pain.

But worst of all was the guilt he felt for allowing himself to be broken by Uzma. The shameful memory of that moment when the words started spilling forth, uncontrollably. Aieron could see The Shadow Master standing over him, Bathamis filling his vision. The Shadow Master's cruel, triumphant laughter filling his ears and echoing through the gem as he prised the information out of him.

Then the recollections of a former life filled his mind. The life of a poor merchant with barely enough money to scrape together a daily meal. A poor life, yet rich with joy.

He met Mirrin and had fallen in love with her. She possessed a strength, the likes of which he had never encountered, not even in The Shadow Master. He followed her and admired her. She transformed him. They spent many a pleasant day together, just the two of them, despite the harsh conditions of their life until, one day; the day Neave arrived in the world.

He remembered the softness of her tiny figure and her startling blue eyes staring up at him. She loved to pull his hair and squeal when he tickled her tummy. He had loved his daughter dearly during this short period of joy in his life. However, The Shadow Master had violently come between them and reclaimed his most trusted spy. These memories had an unfamiliar effect on Aieron. He began to feel. Love and anger intertwined as they rose to the surface and triggered a clarity and resolve in his being.

The Shadow Master severed his life source all those years ago by removing him from the two people in the world he cared about. The anger inside him started to overshadow the love as he remembered plunging a dagger into the heart of his once cherished Mirrin. Uzma used them as tools against each other. That is what hurt Aieron the most. They were but pawns in The Shadow Master's game, nothing more; to be cast aside when he was done with them.

Neave stood in front of him now, skinny, with dirt smeared over her. Such a pitiful creature beside the might of The Shadow Master, but standing fast nonetheless, ever defying his power.

Aieron fought to keep his eyes unfocused to ensure none of this realisation showed on his face. He looked at his daughter. So grown since he had last seen her. That was The Shadow Master's fault too. He could have, should have, been with her, to watch as she grew. Uzma had taken that from him along with everything else. The courage his daughter exuded began to influence his own determination.

Aieron glared up at The Shadow Master sneering down at him and pure hatred seared through him. He did not care anymore if it showed on his face. He snatched the dagger from his belt and with a ferocious snarl launched himself at Uzma. The Shadow Master raised his spear and skewered Aieron through the midriff. Aieron simply grinned, inviting death, then stabbed his knife through Bathamis.

"I am no longer your dog," he whispered.

All the while he laughed at The Shadow Master's expression of horror. He laughed into that grotesque, loathsome, rotting face. He laughed at the irony of the master's tool working so efficiently against him. He was satisfied. He had obtained his revenge. Finally, he was able to let go. He laughed with his final breath as he felt the dagger slip from his grasp and darkness come up to meet him.

Neave watched helplessly as her father's limp body crumpled to the floor and The Shadow Master's sneering smile slipped and was replaced with a look of shock. This expression intensified when Bathamis fell from his eye socket and dropped to the ground and cleaved in two. Neave looked on as if time had slowed as the gem hit the ground and spun in circles before wobbling to a halt. The light faded from its depths and with it the power that it contained. To the unknowing eye, it now resembled a mere stone as any on the mountain side. And as the colour vanished from the gem it was as if a boulder had been lifted from Neave's shoulders. The feeling of despair that had been accumulating over countless days, suddenly dissipated.

She took her chance and ran at The Shadow Master, spear thrust forth. Uzma's weapon was still lodged in her father. It was a hindrance as Uzma tried to wrench it free from under the weight of Aieron's body. He realised it was no use and abandoned his spear, spinning to face Neave with hands ready as she charged towards him. Uzma was too late and the end of Neave's spear was already piercing his throat. He fell backwards; already dead as his body hit the ground. He lay motionless as blood gushed out of his neck and coloured the floor of the cave a deep, dark red. He was gone.

Neave straightened her back and stared about her with an expression of absolute wonder. Everything suddenly felt more real; colours were more vibrant as if a veil had been lifted to reveal the world to her in full. She opened her eyes to a reality that she barely recognised.

Neave watched the other Gwakas. They were all dancing and greeting each other like long lost friends. Her rebels and The Shadow Master's minions alike.

Neave smiled and looked down at the rotting corpse that lay before her. It stank. Neave did not care. It could stink all it liked.

She left her spear sticking out of The Shadow Master's throat – she would no longer need it. She reached down, unhooked the ring of keys hanging at his waist and opened the cage door to free Linken and the others imprisoned. As soon as the door was open, Linken burst forth and wrapped his arms around Neave. He smiled a huge smile as the tears of joy and relief soaked his cheeks.

As she walked toward the fresh breeze that blew gently through the mouth of the cave, Neave passed her father's body and looked down at him in pity. He was still smiling even in death and his eyes no longer had the cast-over look to them. They were pure and true. Neave reached down and closed them. They would do the death rite soon with all the other Gwakas that had died and send their souls to rest. Until it decayed to nourish the earth, his face would bear the scars and his name would forever be tainted with its connection to

Uzma, but soon he would be at rest and that was all that mattered. Neave would make certain that his last deeds did not go unheard.

Neave continued to walk. Beyond the cave mouth she could see that light bathed the land and green plants were cautiously poking their heads out of the ground. Neave drew in a long breath of the fresh, warm air; it had a tinge of sweetness to it. She had lost much, and she knew a period of mourning awaited her, but it would also be a time to mend. Neave reflected on those who had perished on their way to freedom, but she could not bring them back. They had not died in vain. The mountain and valley would bloom again, but it would take years before it reached its true former self.

The Gwakas could not repair themselves like the land. They would forever have the scar of the Shadow days hanging over them. Perhaps in time, they could recover enough to again enjoy the world as they once had. Neave looked up at the blue sky and smiled.

Over time the cave entrance would collapse and bury The Shadow Master's rotting body, and with it, Bathamis.

EPILOGUE

Sage Gwaka sat on his log facing east. The way the sun would have risen if no clouds had covered the sky, casting eternal shadow over the world.

Gry was one of the only humans left alive from the hundreds of people who had once occupied Minethresan valley. He had survived beside the river for a hundred years and seen his world mangle before him. The sight had averted his eyes and made him much accustomed to the appearance of dirt. Not in years had he braved to bear the load of the disfigured land.

Now, finally, Gry looked up from his endless examining of the ground to greet the sun through the parting clouds. As its light spilt over him, he felt his body going rigid and knew that it would not be long.

He had seen an abundance of things in his lifetime, more than he ever wished and had promised himself to see this to the end. He had. But this ending was the mere beginning of a new life.

He blinked once, slowly. A small smile uplifted the corners of his mouth. His body was no more, and his mind was starting to wander, but he wanted to savour this moment. He raised his wrinkled, weathered features to face the rising sun as she finally let her smile shine forth upon the world.

He let go of his physical self and let his soul drift away on the waves of light.

Beside a cliff face, on a stump, a stone statue of a crouching Gwaka sits with face upturned toward the rising sun. In a cave a rotting body lies, and far to the horizon the commoners of Thamisveil cry out in joy and weep for what once was lost but now is found.

ANNI RATTEN

THE SHADOW MASTER'S EYE

www.ingramcontent.com/pod-product-compliance
Lightning Source LLC
Chambersburg PA
CBHW070348130626
46556CB00007B/3079